j537.078 Markle, Sandra.
MAR
   Power up BRANCH

$13.95

DATE			

POWER UP

Books by Sandra Markle

Exploring Winter
Exploring Summer
Science Mini-Mysteries
Power Up

POWER UP

Experiments, Puzzles, and Games
Exploring Electricity

by Sandra Markle

Atheneum   1989   New York

For Rachel, Rebecca, and Stephen (IV),
a lovable group of live wires

Atheneum
Macmillan Publishing Company
866 Third Avenue, New York, NY 10022
Collier Macmillan Canada, Inc.
First Edition   Designed by Eliza Green
Printed in the United States of America

10 9 8 7 6 5 4 3 2 1

Library of Congress Cataloging-in-Publication Data
Markle, Sandra.
Power up: experiments, puzzles, and games exploring electricity/by Sandra Markle.—1st ed.   p.   cm.
Summary: Presents activities to investigate the nature of electricity.
ISBN 0-689-31442-6
1. Electricity—Juvenile literature.   2. Electricity-Experiments—Juvenile literature.
[1. Electricity-Experiments.   2. Experiments.]   I. Title.
QC527.2.M35   1989   537′.07′8—dc 19   88-7772   CIP   AC

The author would like to acknowledge the advice and assistance provided by George Hague, master teaching chair of physical science at St. Mark's School of Texas, Dallas, Texas, 1983 recipient of the presidential award for teaching excellence in science and director for the high school division of the National Science Teachers' Association; W. B. Felegyhazi, manager-battery design for Eveready Battery Company, Inc., Cleveland, Ohio; and Richard H. Dowhan, manager-public affairs for GTE Products Corporation, Danvers, Massachusetts.

Photo illustrations by Bob Byrd, The Light Works, Inc., Dallas, Texas

Contents

Introduction 1

What You'll Need 2

Making Foil Wires 3

Can You Make the Bulb Light Up? 4

How Does a Dry Cell Produce Electricity? 5

The Original Battery 7

How Does Electricity Make a Bulb Light Up? 7

Burned Out 8

A Bright Idea 8

How Incandescent Bulbs Are Made 10

Bulb Search 14

Odd Bulbs 15

To Light or Not to Light 15

A Little Light Work 16

First Aid for Faulty Circuits 18

Conductor Scavenger Hunt 19

Circuit Tester 20

Conductor Deduction 21

The New World of Superconductors 22

Crazy Circuit 23

Circuit Challenge 24

You've Got to Have Connections 25

Lights-On Parade 28

Need a Light? 29

Flashlight Fun 30

How Does a Fuse Work? 30

That's a Switch 33

Blinking Messages 34

The First News Flash 35

Morse Code 35

Circuit Sleuths 36

Conclusion 37

Index 39

POWER UP

Introduction

This book is packed with activities that will let you explore an amazing and powerful force—electricity. You know that electricity can be strong enough to be dangerous. But these experiments, puzzles, and games use the electrical charge produced by a dry cell, which is safe enough to hold in your hand. The special aluminum-foil wires you'll learn how to prepare make experimenting with electrical circuits, bulbs, and switches super-easy as well as safe.

Electricity is a flow of charged particles called electrons. You're probably wondering where these electrons come from. They've been dislodged from atoms, the building blocks of which all matter is made.

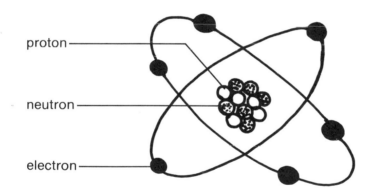

As tiny as they are, each atom is made up of even tinier particles—protons, neutrons, and electrons. The neutrons don't have any charge, but the protons and electrons do. Each proton carries a positive charge and each electron carries a negative charge.

The protons and neutrons form the nucleus of the atom, while the electrons zip around and around this nucleus, orbiting in layers called "shells." The bond holding electrons in orbit is weakest in the outermost shells, so being bumped by a free-moving electron may knock one or more electrons out of the atom's outermost shell. Then these electrons begin to move on their own, possibly bumping into still other atoms and freeing electrons. These electrons flowing together form an electric current.

In the activities that follow, you'll discover how a dry cell produces an electric current. And you'll find out how electricity makes a bulb light up. You'll go hunting for conductors—materials that let electricity flow through them easily. Then you'll use what you've learned about conductors to solve a mystery. You'll investigate two different kinds of circuits, use circuits to create puzzles to challenge your friends, and track down faulty circuits. You'll also make a flashlight and construct a special telegraph you can use to send messages.

Ready for action? Then collect the supplies listed below and get started.

What You'll Need

aluminum foil
steel paper clips
1.5-volt flashlight bulbs
Styrofoam peanuts
metal spoon
poster board
rubber cement
scissors

D-cells
glass
wooden ice-cream stick
empty toilet-paper tube
3 x 5 index cards
cellophane tape (or pack-
    aging or masking tape)
pennies

paper towels
orthodontic rubber bands
construction paper
tracing paper (or thin
    writing paper)
steel wool
empty soft drink can
pencil

You may think of the D-cells as batteries. They're commonly called that. Technically, though, each D-cell is a dry cell. And the term *battery* is reserved for a group of dry cells functioning together. Throughout the activities in this book, you'll find D-cells referred to as dry cells.

Warning: The amount of electricity given off by D-cells—even when several are used together—isn't enough to harm you. The amount of electricity available through a wall plug, a light socket, or any other electrical outlet, though, is DANGEROUS. So never try plugging any of your experimental equipment into one of these.

Making Foil Wires

You're going to need lots of wire to make connections as you investigate. And you can make some super, easy-to-use wires using aluminum foil and tape. Start by tearing off a sheet of aluminum foil about twelve to fourteen inches long. Next, tear off strips of three-quarter- or one-inch-wide cellophane tape, masking tape, or packaging tape as long as the foil sheet. Stick as many of these strips as you can side by side on the *dull* side of the foil, without having them touch, and cut on either side of the tape to form foil ribbons. Then fold each ribbon in half lengthwise, so the taped side is inside. Run your fingers along each shiny ribbon to crease it, pressing the two taped sides together.

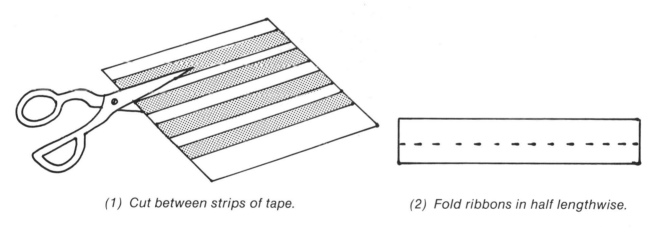

(1) Cut between strips of tape.

(2) Fold ribbons in half lengthwise.

As you experiment, you may discover that you need some longer wire. Simply use steel paper clips to hook two or more wires together. Or if you find you need shorter wire, just snip off a piece so the wire's the right length.

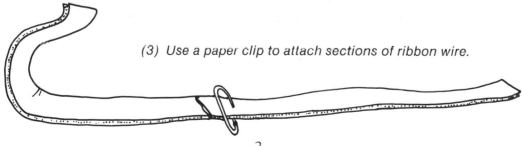

(3) Use a paper clip to attach sections of ribbon wire.

Can You Make the Bulb Light Up?

See if you can figure out how to put these items together in a way that will make the bulb light up. You'll find one possible solution on page 6. After you've experimented, read the explanation below.

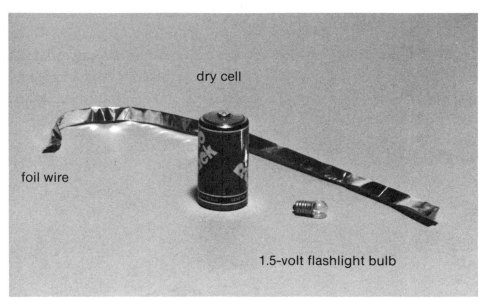

dry cell

foil wire

1.5-volt flashlight bulb

Why It Happened: You probably know that a dry cell produces electricity. Games, toys, radios, and lots of other things use this power source. And you know light bulbs need electricity to light up. That's why a lamp won't light unless it's plugged into an electrical outlet. But you may be surprised to discover that it's not enough to send electrons from a power source to a light bulb. In order for electricity to flow through the bulb and make it light up, there also needs to be a path from the light bulb back to the power source. That's why an electrical plug has two main prongs. And that's why you had to connect the bulb's two contact points (side of the base and center-bottom tip of the base) to the dry cell's two contact points (the two ends). The pathway you created for the electrons to follow is called a *complete circuit*. And only a complete circuit will make a light bulb light up.

How Does a Dry Cell Produce Electricity?

Electricity is produced as the result of a chemical reaction. Look closely at the sliced-open dry cell in the photo. The reaction takes place between the zinc atoms and the manganese dioxide atoms. When zinc reacts with manganese dioxide, the zinc atoms lose electrons and the manganese dioxide atoms absorb those electrons. The freely moving electrons en route between the zinc and manganese dioxide form an electric current. As the manganese dioxide atoms gain electrons, they become manganese oxide atoms and are unable to absorb any more electrons. When all the zinc and manganese dioxide atoms have reacted, no more electricity is produced, and the dry cell is said to be "dead."

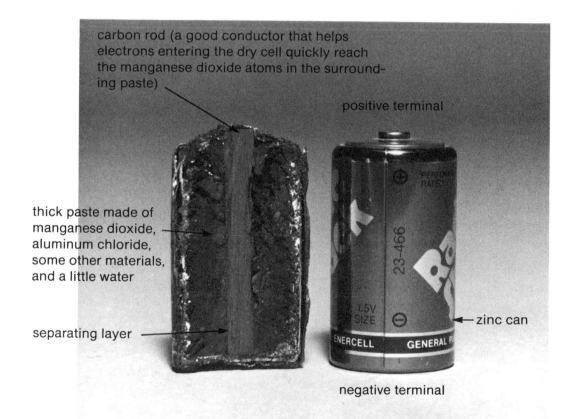

carbon rod (a good conductor that helps electrons entering the dry cell quickly reach the manganese dioxide atoms in the surrounding paste)

positive terminal

thick paste made of manganese dioxide, aluminum chloride, some other materials, and a little water

23-466

1.5V SIZE

ENERCELL   GENERAL

zinc can

separating layer

negative terminal

If the zinc and the manganese dioxide were in direct contact with each other, this reaction would happen very quickly and soon be finished. So when a dry cell is assembled, a separation layer—usually in the form of a piece of paper—is inserted between these two materials. This doesn't totally stop the reaction. That's why a dry cell will eventually go dead even if it's never used. But, since the paper resists the flow of electrons through it, the reaction is greatly slowed down.

In a complete circuit, a wire made of a material—such as aluminum or copper—that lets electrons flow through it easily provides an easy pathway between the zinc and the manganese dioxide atoms. This route requires the electrons to travel farther. They may even have to pass through a light bulb, a radio, an electric toy car, or some other electric device along the way. But because electrons can move along this pathway so quickly, the chemical reaction happens much faster.

When the dry cell is connected in a complete circuit, the electron flow produces a pressure or electromotive force similar to the pressure created by water moving through a hose. This pressure is measured in what are called volts. A single dry cell like the one in the photo on page 12 generates about 1.5 volts of electricity when it's connected in a complete circuit.

Now that you know how a dry cell generates electricity, you can see why disconnecting a circuit when electricity isn't actually needed helps the dry cell to last longer. Can you figure out why storing dry cells not in use at low temperatures, such as in a refrigerator, also extends their life?

Can You Make the Bulb Light Up? Solution:

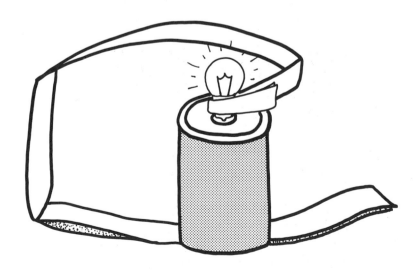

The Original Battery

Alessandro Volta (1745-1827), an Italian physicist, first successfully used a chemical reaction to generate electricity in 1795. Volta, however, used zinc and silver plates separated by paper or cloth dipped in salt water. Imagine how heavy—and messy—it would be to carry one of Volta's electrical cells as a power source for your portable radio!

How Does Electricity Make a Bulb Light Up?

In the diagram, you can see that one end of the thin wire, or filament, is connected to each of the bulb's contact points. Electricity can flow in the bottom contact and out the side. Or it can flow in the side contact and out the bottom. The important thing is that there is a flow of electrons through the thin filament. This filament is made of a material that resists the flow of electrons through it. Rub your hands together hard. Feel the heat from this friction? Resistance causes friction in the bulb's filament and heats it up hot enough to glow.

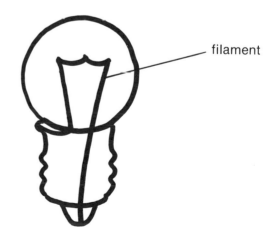

filament

Burned Out

Have you ever turned on a bulb, had it suddenly shine, and then go out? If you'd looked closely at this burned-out bulb, you'd have seen that the filament had a piece missing. Remember, you just learned that the light bulb glows because this wire gets very hot. The inside of the bulb doesn't contain any oxygen. And since oxygen is needed to make something burn, the filament never bursts into flames. Each time the filament gets hot enough to glow, though, a little of the metal evaporates. This material may form a dark coating on the inside of the bulb. More importantly, every bit that is lost makes the filament thinner. Eventually, the filament gets so thin it breaks, breaking the circuit.

A Bright Idea

As soon as experimentors figured out how to generate electricity, they began to investigate how this power could be used to produce light. In fact as early as 1802, experimentors had been able to test what happened when an electric current passed through thin strips of metal. The metal quickly became hot and glowed, or became incandescent. But the light only lasted a few seconds because the metal strip melted. It wasn't until 1879 that the American inventor Thomas Alva Edison (1847–1931) succeeded in creating an incandescent light bulb that could be counted on to glow long enough to be used as a practical source of light.

One thing Edison discovered as he experimented on the light bulb was that it helped to eliminate the oxygen around the filament, since fire needs oxygen to burn. The less oxygen there was, the longer the glowing-hot filament took to burn up. So Edison learned to mount his test filament in a glass jar and then pump out the air with a hand vacuum pump, creating at least a partial vacuum.

The hardest part of producing a reliable incandescent bulb, though, was finding a suitable material for the filament. It had to have a high melting temperature, but be able to glow white-hot. Edison tried a lot of different materials. (Tungsten, the material most often used for filaments today, wasn't available at that time in a form that could be worked into a thin filament.) Then, on October 21, 1879, Edison set up a bulb made with a simple, carbonized cotton sewing thread as a filament. To his surprise, it not only burned more than a few minutes, but kept on glowing for almost forty hours.

Forty hours, though, wasn't enough for Edison. He wanted to produce a bulb with a lifetime of over four hundred hours. So, with the help of his staff, he proceeded to carbonize and test everything he could get his hands on—cardboard, grasses, various kinds of wood. Over six thousand different kinds of materials were tried. At last, Edison found a type of bamboo whose fibers made the long-lasting filaments he wanted. In 1880, in one of the first commercial tests of these new bulbs, several hundred lights were installed aboard an ocean steamer, the SS *Columbia*. This ship sailed from San Francisco, California, to New York City, around the Cape of Good Hope. And during this entire long sea voyage, not one light bulb burned out.

Of course, just developing a long-lasting light bulb wasn't enough. To make electric lights available to the public, Edison had to design electric lines, a power-generating station—even lamps, sockets, and switches. In 1882, Edison put the first generating station into operation in New York City. It was a success, but it only generated enough power to light up ten city blocks. The next time you're out at night, look around at all the glowing lights in homes, on big buildings, and illuminating streets and parks. And think about a time when only ten blocks in one city of the United States had electric lights.

This picture of Thomas Edison with several early light bulbs was taken in his laboratory (West Orange, New Jersey) in 1917. Notice the bulb hanging down behind Edison.

How Incandescent Bulbs Are Made

Until 1912, the glass envelope for each bulb was separately hand blown. Next, the air was drawn out through a tube fastened to the rounded end. Once the vacuum was complete, this tube was sealed with a flame and snipped off, leaving a sharp, fragile tip that made shipping the bulb very difficult.

In Edison's very first light bulb, the base was simply a wooden platform to which wires were connected. And the bulb was cemented in place. The first screw base was developed in 1880, but this also was made out of wood. A later plaster of paris base was only a slight improvement, since it cracked easily if the bulb was screwed in too tightly. Then, in the early 1900s, the brass screw base was developed. This worked well, but there was still a problem. Finding a replacement bulb to fit each lamp was difficult because light-bulb bases came in as many as sixteen different styles. In fact, those early bulbs were often recycled.

When the bulb burned out, it was shipped back to the manufacturer or to a company that handled recycling bulbs. There, the bulb's pointed tip was snipped off, the old filament was removed, and a new filament was inserted. Then the air was once again sucked out, creating a vacuum, and a dab of hot glass resealed the bulb.

Early incandescent bulbs
COURTESY OF GTE PRODUCTS CORP.

Today, light-bulb sizes and base shapes are basically uniform, and light-bulb production is highly automated. To produce the glass envelopes, a ribbon machine takes a continuous stream of molten glass from a furnace, presses it into a ribbon, and blows this ribbon into molds.

A ribbon machine may produce as many as one thousand bulbs every minute.
COURTESY OF GE LIGHTING, CLEVELAND.

Meanwhile, the mount machine is preparing what will go inside the glass envelope. First, the stem is assembled. The stem consists of glass tubing—part of which will be used to draw air out of the bulb—and lead-in wires. Some bulbs also may have special wires to support the filament. Next, the filament is attached to the stem. The filament is usually a coil of tungsten wire. When finished, the mounts are delivered by a conveyer belt to the sealing and exhaust machine.

11

An early light-bulb manufacturing plant   COURTESY OF GTE PRODUCTS CORP.

This machine lowers a glass bulb that is just the right size over each mount, and a gas flame seals the bulb's neck. Next, air inside the bulb is drawn out through the exhaust tube. Bulbs under forty watts are usually left with a vacuum. Bulbs designed for greater wattage, though, are filled with a special mixture of nitrogen and argon gases. The gas mixture conducts away some of the heat given off by the glowing filament. This keeps the filament from getting as hot as it might, and the bulb glows a little less brightly than it could. But, less heat also makes the filament evaporate more slowly. And this makes the bulb last longer.

Finally, bulbs and bases, prefilled with cement, are transferred to the finishing machine. Here each bulb is plugged into a base, and the lead-in wires are soldered to the two contact points. Then the bulbs are tested, and if they work, they're packaged for sale.

Light bulbs on a conveyor belt COURTESY OF GTE PRODUCTS CORP.

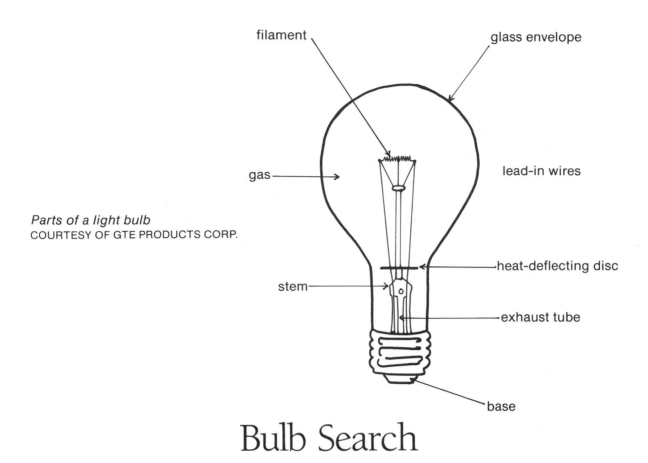

filament

glass envelope

gas

lead-in wires

Parts of a light bulb
COURTESY OF GTE PRODUCTS CORP.

heat-deflecting disc

stem

exhaust tube

base

Bulb Search

How many different kinds of light bulbs can you find around your house? Look for each of the types shown below. Then see what other kinds of light bulbs you can find. If all the light bulbs in your house were to burn out at one time, how many bulbs would you need to replace?

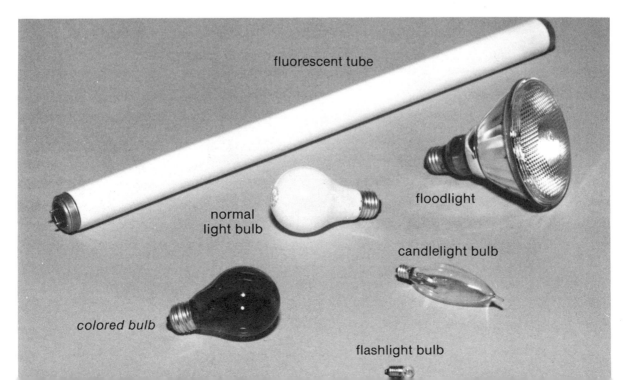

fluorescent tube

floodlight

normal
light bulb

candlelight bulb

colored bulb

flashlight bulb

Odd Bulbs

One of the tiniest bulbs ever produced was called the grain-of-wheat bulb because it was about the size of a single grain of wheat. Each little light bulb was only 0.33 inch long and weighed 0.05 grams. Wondering why anyone would need such a tiny light? Doctors used the grain-of-wheat bulb to help them perform delicate surgical operations on children.

The world's largest bulb, on the other hand, never had a practical use. It was created just for display in 1954, during the Electric Light's Diamond Jubilee, a celebration honoring Edison's development of the first practical incandescent bulb. But what a light this giant was! The bulb was twenty inches in diameter, forty-two inches high, and weighed fifty pounds. If its tungsten filament had been uncoiled, it would have stretched out twelve and one-half feet. It's no wonder that when this bulb was switched on, no one could safely look directly at it. To view its brilliance, spectators had to turn their backs on the bulb and look at its reflection in a special window. This single bulb gave off as much light as 2,875 sixty-watt household bulbs all burning simultaneously.

To Light or Not to Light?

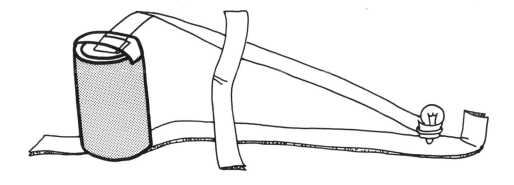

Look at the circuit pictured on page 17. Will it make the light bulb light up? Why or why not? (**Clue:** Trace the path the electrons would follow through this circuit.) To check yourself, collect two regular foil wires, a short foil wire, a D-cell, cellophane tape, a 1.5-volt flashlight bulb, and an orthodontic rubber band. Follow the steps to build and test the circuit. Then read the explanation below.

1. Lay one foil wire on a table. Set the dry cell—negative terminal down—on this wire. Next, fold a tab at one end of the other regular foil wire. Place this over the positive terminal and secure it with a tape strip.
2. Fold the free end of the wire attached to the positive terminal to make it narrower. Next, wrap this end around the bulb's base and secure it with the rubber band.
3. When you're ready to see what happens in this circuit, first touch the tip of the bulb's base to the foil wire lying on the table. The bulb will light up. Then lay the short foil wire across the two long wires as shown. And observe what happens to the bulb.

Why It Happened: Did you correctly guess that the pictured circuit won't make the bulb light up? This is what's called a *short circuit*, meaning that the electrons are able to follow a shorter path back to the power source rather than follow the longer path that goes through the bulb's filament. A frayed wire can cause a short circuit. Electrical wiring is coated with an insulator to keep the electrons flowing along a specific route. If the insulation is broken, a wire may touch another wire or even another loop of itself. If this provides a shorter path back to the power source, the electrons will take it.

A Little Light Work

Ready for a challenge? Then predict which of the circuits pictured on the next page will make the bulb light up. You can check yourself by building and testing each of the circuits. Or check the answer on page 18.

A

B

C

D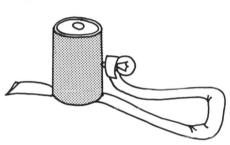

E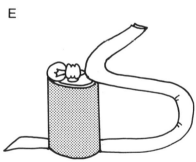

F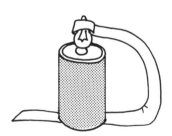

17

First Aid for Faulty Circuits

If a circuit you build doesn't light the bulb, don't panic. Check for these problems:

1. Is something loose, keeping a contact point from being connected? Remember the dry cell has two contact points and the bulb has two contact points—and all four of these contact points must be connected to the circuit.

2. Is there a short circuit?

3. Is electricity flowing from the negative terminal to the positive terminal? If you've connected more than one dry cell to the circuit, check to be sure that a negative terminal is always in contact with a positive terminal. Remember, the electric current only flows in one direction when dry cells are connected in a circuit.

4. Is there a faulty component? Use a circuit that you can see is working successfully. Substitute parts from the faulty circuit for those in the working circuit—one part at a time—to make sure the light bulb, the dry cell, or even a foil wire isn't the source of the problem.

A Little Light Work Solutions: Circuits B and E are complete circuits and will light up the bulb. The others are incomplete circuits.

Why did Sally take back her new electric alarm clock?
It kept going off while she was asleep.

Conductor Scavenger Hunt

Some materials let electrons move through them easily. These are called *conductors*. Other materials resist electron flow. These are called *insulators*.

Do you know which of the items listed below are conductors? You can find out with a circuit tester. Directions for building a circuit tester and using it to test for conductors are provided on page 20.

stainless steel knife	tennis shoe's rubber sole	glass
candle	metal door knob	cotton T-shirt
penny	braces on somebody's teeth	paper napkin
plastic button	wooden ice-cream stick	metal zipper
toothbrush bristles	clay flowerpot	metal faucet

Can you find any other conductors around your house? (Remember, *never* try to attach any of your experimental equipment to an electrical outlet or socket.) What kind of material were all the conductors made of?

Why did the traffic light turn red?
So would you if you had to change in front of all those people.

Circuit Tester

Collect a foil wire, a D-cell, cellophane tape, and a flashlight bulb. Start by folding over one end of the wire about three times to make a tab. Place this tab tightly against the negative terminal and secure it with a strip of tape. Next, fold the free end of the wire to make it narrower and wrap this end around the light bulb's base.

Test each item by bringing it in contact with both the dry cell's positive terminal and the bulb's bottom tip. If the item is made of a material that is a conductor, electrons will flow between these two contact points, creating a complete circuit. And the bulb will light up.

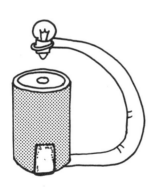

Conductor Deduction

Just before closing time, two men wearing Halloween masks and carrying guns burst into the First Citizens Savings and Loan. Within minutes, they had collected the bank's cash. Next, they ushered John Tyler, the bank manager, Evelyn White, the bank teller, and an elderly couple, the bank's last remaining customers, into the vault. Flipping open the panel for the emergency circuit—the one designed to let someone locked inside the vault open the door—one of the robbers yanked out a nearly foot-long piece of wire, breaking this circuit. Then he closed the vault door.

In the silence that followed, the frightened group stood trembling, staring at each other. At last, Evelyn White voiced what they all knew. "We're trapped," she announced.

"How long before…before we run out of air?" the elderly gentleman asked, putting his arm around his wife.

"Perhaps we won't need to wait to be rescued." Tyler smiled. "Perhaps there's something we can use in place of the wire so we can activate the emergency circuit." Here's a photo of the pile of things the group was able to collect among themselves. Can you spot a conductor that could be used to span the twelve-inch gap and complete the broken circuit? Use the circuit tester to test your idea. Then check yourself by reading the solution on page 22.

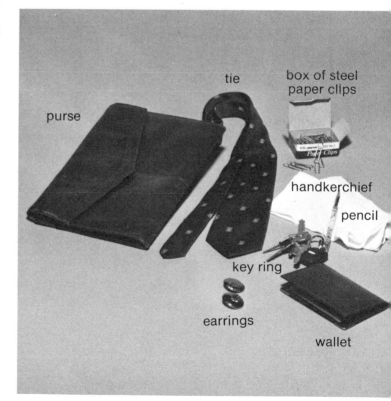

purse · tie · box of steel paper clips · handkerchief · pencil · key ring · earrings · wallet

The New World of Superconductors

While conductors let electricity slip through much more easily than nonconductors do, there is still some resistance. At least a few of the electrons bump into atoms within the material along the way. These collisions produce heat, plus a loss of at least a little electrical power.

While a little lost electricity may not seem like much, sometimes it's critical. So scientists learned that they could supercool conductors, creating superconductors. Supercooling was also superexpensive, though. So superconductors were impractical at first.

Then, in 1986, research by a number of different scientists led to the discovery of a type of ceramic—similar to the kind used to make dinner plates—that would act as a superconductor at only -283°F. That may sound very chilly to you, but it's one hundred degrees warmer than what had been possible in earlier experiments.

Since cooling is now easier and cheaper to do, lots of new uses are being considered for superconductors. One possible application will be to produce a high-speed train that will use superconducting magnets to float the train above a track. Experimental models of this magnetically raised train, called the Maglev and built in Japan, can travel three hundred miles per hour without producing any noise or vibrations.

Conductor Deduction Solution: John Tyler hooked together enough of the steel paper clips to span the distance and complete the circuit. In fact, the group got out of the vault so quickly that they were able to call the police in time for the robbers to be caught only a block from the bank.

Crazy Circuit

Here's your chance to let your creativity shine. Because anything that is a good conductor will let electricity pass through easily, a complete circuit could actually be made with things other than just wires. First, decide which of the items shown below are good condutors. (**Clue:** Use the circuit tester you built for the conductor scavenger hunt to test any you aren't sure about.) Next, collect all these items plus two foil wires, a 1.5-volt flashlight bulb, and two D-cells. Then find a way to connect all the good conductors, the dry cells, and the light bulb together to build a circuit that will light up the bulb. Although there are lots of possibilities, you'll find one possible solution on page 25.

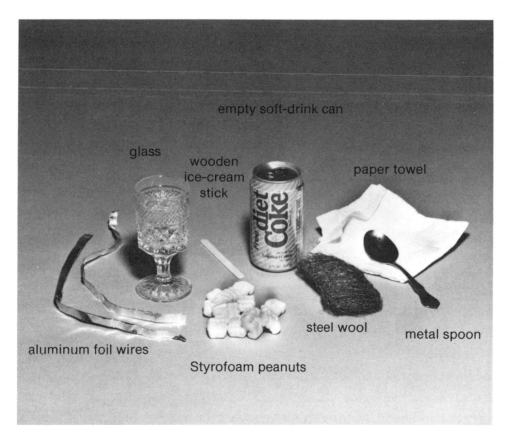

Circuit Challenge

You can build a puzzle to challenge your friends. First, pick a topic, such as facts about major cities or basketball records. Then, do a little research to write five questions and answers about the topic. Next, cut a sheet of poster board the size of a sheet of notebook paper. Punch five holes, equally spaced, down the left-hand side of the poster board. Punch five more holes directly across from the first set down the right-hand side of the poster board. Number one through five beside the left-hand set of holes and write one question next to each number. Then write an answer for one of the questions opposite each question. But be sure the answers are mixed up. In other words, the answer opposite question number one might actually be the answer for question number four, and so forth.

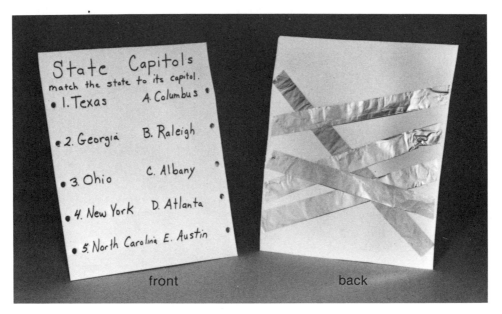

front   back

To finish your puzzle, cut strips of aluminum foil that are about a half-inch wide. On the back of the poster board, stretch an aluminum foil strip—shiny side down—from each question hole to the hole next to the correct answer for that question. Use tape to anchor each strip in place. Be sure the foil completely covers the hole so that, from the front, the holes appear as aluminum foil spots. It's okay to have the foil strips crisscross each other.

Finally, cut another piece of poster board the same size as the first. Lay it over the back—to hide the foil strips—and tape the edges. Then get a circuit tester (see page 20) and challenge a friend to solve the puzzle. When an answer is guessed, touch the positive terminal to the question hole and the tip of the bulb's base to the answer hole. If the answer is correct, the circuit will be complete and the bulb will light up. Bright answer!

Crazy Circuit Solution: Be sure to include these conductors in your circuit: soft-drink can, metal spoon, and steel wool. You may find other circuits that work, but here's one possible solution.

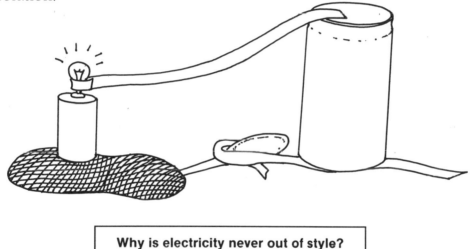

> **Why is electricity never out of style?**
> Because it's always current.

You've Got to Have Connections

You already know that a light bulb won't light unless there is a complete circuit. But you may be surprised to discover that there are two different ways dry cells or bulbs can be connected in a complete circuit—in series or in parallel. To find out how these are different, follow the directions below to build each type of circuit. Then see if you can solve the challenges. You can check yourself by testing the circuits. Then be sure to read the explanation on page 27.

25

In Series: You'll need three D-cells, a foil wire, cellophane tape, an orthodontic rubber band, and a 1.5-volt flashlight bulb.

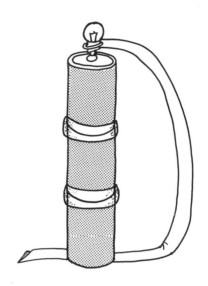

1. Lay the foil wire on the table. Set the negative terminal of one dry cell on this wire near one end.
2. Stack the second and third dry cells on top of the first—negative terminals in contact with positive terminals. Use tape to hold the dry cells together.
3. Fold the free end of the wire to make it narrower and wrap that end around the bulb's base. Anchor it with an orthodontic rubber band. When you want to complete the circuit and light up the bulb, touch the tip of the bulb's base to the positive terminal of the top dry cell.

In Parallel: You'll need three D-cells, two foil wires, an orthodontic rubber band, and a 1.5-volt flashlight bulb.

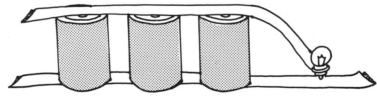

1. Lay one foil wire on the table. Set the three dry cells side by side—negative terminals down—on this wire.
2. Fold one end of the other wire to make it narrower and wrap that end around the bulb's base. Anchor it with the rubber band.
3. Stretch the wire with the bulb attached across the dry cells' positive terminals one at a time, pressing the contact in place with a finger and anchoring it with a strip of tape. When you want to complete the circuit and light up the bulb, touch the tip of the bulb's base to the wire the dry cells are sitting on.

Note: Be sure to build your circuits with brand-new D-cells so you can count on them to be strong.

Challengers

Now, use what you discovered to answer these questions. Then check yourself by reading the explanations below.

1. Do you think the light bulb will shine brighter when the dry cells are connected in series or in parallel? Or will it shine equally bright in both circuits?
2. Will removing one dry cell break the circuit and make the bulb go out when the dry cells are connected in series? Remember, when you remove a dry cell, don't change the spacing. It will help you to predict what will happen if you think about the path the electrons would follow through the circuit.
3. Will removing one dry cell break the circuit and make the bulb go out when the dry cells are connected in parallel? Think again about the electrons' path through the circuit.
4. Light bulbs also may be wired in series or in parallel. Strings of Christmas-tree lights usually have the bulbs wired in parallel. Why do you suppose they are wired that way rather than in series?

Why It Happened

1. The light bulb is noticeably brighter when the dry cells are connected in series. The reason this happens is that when the dry cells are connected in series, the electrons move through the circuit with greater electromotive force. Having the dry cells connected in parallel, on the other hand, increases the number of electrons flowing through the circuit. But the force of the electron flow isn't any greater than it would be if the light bulb was only connected to one dry cell. Since it's a resistance to the electron flow that makes the filament get hot enough to glow, increasing the electromotive force of electrons moving through the filament makes the light bulb shine more brightly. Simply increasing the number of electrons flowing through the circuit, on the other hand, doesn't effect how brightly the bulb shines.
2. There must be a complete pathway through both contact points of each dry cell, as well as through both of the bulb's contact points. With one dry cell—any of the three—missing, the circuit is broken.
3. The light won't go out this time. The difference is that each dry cell has its two contact points directly in contact with the foil wire, so electrons flow out the negative terminal of each dry cell and back to the positive terminal just as if this was the only dry cell in the circuit.

4. If a string of Christmas-tree lights was wired in series, just one burned-out bulb would break the circuit and make all the bulbs go out. Think how hard it would be to determine which bulb was burned out if there were a hundred bulbs in the string!

Lights-On Parade

Each night during summer vacations and spring breaks, visitors to the Disney theme parks are treated to a display of electrical whimsy. Nearly six thousand tiny bulbs adorn this approximately sixteen-foot-tall, forty-foot-long magical beast. And Pete's dragon, a character from one of the Disney movies, is only one of thirty floats that dazzle visitors with almost a million twinkling lights. Twenty six-volt batteries, similar to automobile batteries, are needed just to make the dragon light up. And additional banks of batteries provide power for the float's sound equipment and the special vehicle that propels the dragon during the parade.

During the day, the giant floats sit inside a warehouse-size storage area, each plugged into rechargers. Ten to twelve hours are needed to fully recharge the banks of batteries. Meanwhile, the maintenance crew checks for burned-out bulbs.

Wondering how many bulbs stop glowing when a single bulb burns out on one of these floats? The answer is seven. The floats' lights are wired both in series and in parallel. Having all the bulbs wired in series would mean that one burned-out bulb would darken the whole float. The individual bulbs are so small, though, that spotting one burned-out bulb can be tough. So, groups of seven bulbs are wired in series. And the floats are covered with many sets wired in parallel.

Pete's dragon

Need a Light?

You can build your own flashlight. You'll need an empty toilet-paper tube, a 1.5-volt flashlight bulb, a sheet of construction paper, a sheet of tracing paper or thin writing paper, a pencil, scissors, aluminum foil, rubber cement, cellophane tape, and a twelve-inch-long aluminum foil wire.

Start by tracing the outline on this page. Then cut this pattern out of both construction paper and the aluminum foil. Use rubber cement to attach the dull side of the foil to the paper. Then, holding one side of the circle at the slit, slide it across the other side to form a funnel. The small hole at the bottom should be just big enough for the base of the bulb to poke through. Tape the sides of the cone where they overlap, to hold them in place.

Next, put one dry cell into the paper tube—negative terminal down. Set the second dry cell on top of the first—indented end down. Thread the foil wire inside the tube along one side and pull the end of the wire across the bottom dry cell. Crisscross strips of tape to hold the foil wire in contact with the indented end of the dry cell and to keep the dry cells from falling out of the tube.

Finally, thread the free end of the foil wire through the funnel's small hole. Fold the end of the wire to make it narrower and wrap this end around the base of the bulb. Next, push the bulb's base through the small funnel hole.

Ready to switch on your homemade flashlight? Hold the tube containing the dry cells in one hand and the paper cone in the other. Then, complete the circuit you built by touching the tip of the bulb's base to the knob end of the top dry cell.

**Why did the light bulb ask so
many questions?**
It was a 100-watt (what) bulb.

Flashlight Fun

In a dimly lit room, experiment with the shadows you can create using your homemade flashlight. Shine the light at an object. How long can you make its shadow stretch? Can you change the shadow's shape by changing the way you aim the flashlight at the object?

Or put on a shadow-puppet show. First, cut solid shapes out of stiff cardboard and tape each one onto a wooden ruler or wooden paint-stirring stick. Next, hang a sheet over the side of a table. Then crawl in behind the sheet. You'll need a helper. While you put your puppet into action, your helper will need to shine the flashlight directly at the sheet from behind the puppet. The audience will see the shadow figure on the sheet screen. By moving the puppet closer to the screen or farther away from it, you can change the size and appearance of the projected image. See what special effects you can create.

How Does a Fuse Work?

A fuse is an important safety device. The wire in a fuse melts when the flow of electricity through it becomes greater than the load it's designed to handle. And when the fuse melts, the circuit is broken. So everything that was running on electricity shuts down, electricity stops flowing, and the wires cool off. This blackout can be annoying. But if it didn't happen, the excessive load of electricity would make the wiring get hotter and hotter. It might even get hot enough to start a fire.

You can make a model fuse to see for yourself how one works. You'll need an index card, scissors, cellophane tape, steel wool, two pennies, two D-cells, a 1.5-volt flashlight bulb, an orthodontic rubber band, a regular foil wire, and a foil wire about six inches long.

First, cut off one-fourth of the index card. Tease out one short steel-wool wire, stretch this across the card, and tape either end. Don't worry if the wire isn't pulled tight or straight. Next, place the two pennies on the steel-wool wire so the distance between them is just enough to slip a steel paper clip through when it's turned on edge. Use tape to anchor the right-hand penny, but be careful to cover as little of the coin as possible. Lay one end of the short foil wire on top of the left-hand penny and tape it the same way.

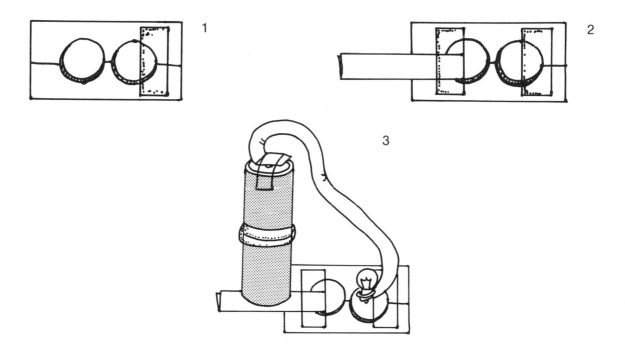

Next, stack two of the D-cells, making sure the negative terminal of the top cell is in contact with the positive terminal of the bottom cell. Use tape to hold the two together. Fold a tab on one end of the long foil wire, place it over the positive terminal of the top dry cell, and anchor it with tape. Fold the other end of this wire to make it narrower, wrap this end around the bulb's base, and secure it with an orthodontic rubber band.

When you're ready to activate the fuse, set the dry cells, negative terminal down, on the short wire. Be sure the dry cells are pressed together so the contact points are touching. Then touch the tip of the bulb's base to the part of the right-hand penny that's exposed. The bulb will light up. Watch the steel-wool wire closely. There'll be a tiny spark. This is the wire melting. And when the circuit is broken, the bulb will go dark.

If the fuse doesn't melt quickly, try one of these two things:
1. Reposition the pennies closer together, making the fuse even shorter.
2. Add a third dry cell to the stack, increasing the flow of electricity through the circuit.

A stronger-than-normal flow of electricity can occur when too many appliances that use electricity are plugged into a circuit. A short circuit—electricity bypassing the route it should take through appliances—can also increase the flow of electricity to a dangerous level. Check your home for overloaded circuits—one with extension cords or special plugs that allow several items to be plugged in at one time. Also look for frayed electrical cords because these could cause "shorts." Report any problems you find to an adult.

Ask your parents to show you the fuse box for your home. And look at a fuse close up. Many of them have a little window so you can see if the wire inside has melted. Fuses come in a variety of current ratings—meaning how much electricity the fuse can carry before the wire inside melts. Sometimes people have replaced burned-out fuses with a penny. This works because a penny is made of copper, a good conductor. Why is using a penny to replace a fuse a very foolish thing to do?

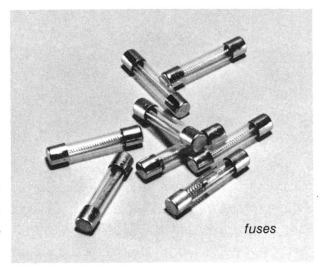

fuses

In many newer homes, circuit breakers are used instead of fuses. A circuit breaker is an automatic switch designed to let only a certain amount of electric current pass. If that limit is exceeded, the automatic mechanism—usually electromagnets or a temperature-sensitive device similar to that used in a furnace thermostat—throws open a set of contacts. And, like the melting fuse wire, this breaks the circuit, stopping the flow of electricity.

That's a Switch!

A switch is a device that makes it easy to complete or break a circuit. To build a simple switch, collect a D-cell, two regular foil wires, a foil wire about three inches long, cellophane tape, a 1.5-volt flashlight bulb, an orthodontic rubber band, and an index card.

First, fold one end of each of the two regular foil wires to form a tab, press one tab tightly against each of the dry cell's terminals, and secure these with tape. Next, fold the free end of the wire attached to the negative terminal to make it narrower and wrap this end around the bulb's base. Anchor it in place with the rubber band. Then, lay the end of the short foil wire on the index card. Secure it by placing a strip of tape along one edge.

Hold the tip of the bulb's base in contact with the short foil wire. Then slide the free end of the foil wire attached to the dry cell's positive terminal under the free end of the short foil wire.

The short foil wire is the switch. When you want to complete the circuit and light up the bulb, press this wire down so it's in contact with the foil wire under it. When you want to break the circuit and turn off the bulb, lift up this switch.

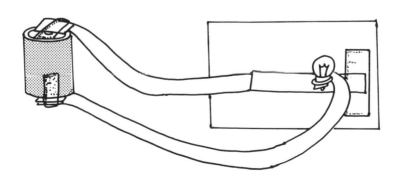

Blinking Messages

The telegraph revolutionized communication by making it possible to send messages long distances almost instantly. Before the telegraph, a message depended on a man on horseback, a train, or even a boat to carry it to its destination.

You can make a type of telegraph to send messages to a friend. Each person who will be sending messages will need to construct one of these light telegraphs. To build one light telegraph, you'll need a D-cell, four foil wires, three steel paper clips, cellophane tape, a 1.5-volt flashlight bulb, and an orthodontic rubber band.

Start by folding the end of one foil wire to form a tab. Place this firmly over the dry cell's negative terminal and tape it in place. Tape the end of another foil wire to the side of the dry cell, as shown below. Slip a paper clip over this wire where it can easily come into contact with the dry cell's positive terminal. Next, use paper clips to add an extension to each of the two wires. (Add more extension wires if the person receiving the messages needs to be farther away.)

Fold the free end of the wire attached to the side of the dry cell to make it narrower. Wrap this around the bulb's base and secure it with the rubber band.

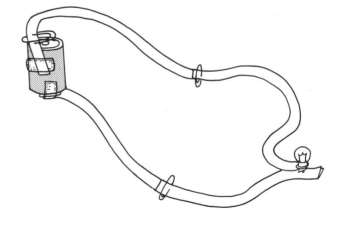

The person receiving the message will hold the tip of the bulb's base against the wire connected to the negative terminal. The person sending the message will touch the paper clip to the positive terminal to complete the circuit. Each time the circuit is completed, the bulb will light up. (If the bulb doesn't light, check **First Aid for Faulty Circuits** on page 18.) Touching the paper clip to the positive terminal only briefly before lifting it to break the circuit will make the bulb blink. Holding the paper clip against this terminal longer will make the bulb flash.

Samuel Morse, inventor of the telegraph, also developed an alphabet of dots and dashes. Morse's telegraph used short and long clicks. But you can use Morse code and your light telegraph to spell out words in blinks and flashes.

The First News Flash

Although Samuel Morse first drew up the plans for the telegraph in 1832, it took him years of experimenting to perfect this instrument. He also had to develop a special alphabet, Morse code, that could be used to send messages with electric signals. Then Morse had to convince the public that the telegraph was a worthwhile invention. An opportunity to do that came when the Democratic Convention met in Baltimore, Maryland, in 1844.

President Van Buren was expected to get the nomination to run for reelection. But when the convention voted, Van Buren didn't receive the two-thirds majority he needed to win. So a heated debate followed. And when it was finished, James K. Polk was nominated as the party's presidential candidate. One of Morse's assistants quickly transmitted this surprise news to Samuel Morse, waiting in Washington, D.C. And he spread the news. When the reporters arrived by train an hour later with what they thought was a scoop, they were shocked to discover everyone had already heard about Polk's nomination.

Morse Code

A .－	G －－.	M －－	S ...
B －...	H	N －.	T －
C －.－.	I ..	O －－－	U ..－
D －..	J .－－－	P .－－.	V ...－
E .	K －.－	Q －－.－	W .－－
F ..－.	L .－..	R .－.	X －..－
			Y －.－－
			Z －－..

Comma －－..－－

Period .－.－.

Over (meaning you want a reply) －.－

Out (meaning your message is complete) .－.－.

Circuit Sleuths

Only one of the circuits shown below will make the bulb light up. Can you find that circuit? And can you figure out how to fix each of the other faulty circuits?

Whoops—those probably don't look like circuits to you. Because drawing pictures of dry cells, bulbs, and switches can take a lot of time, special symbols are used to represent each of these. Look at the symbol guide in the box to understand what each circuit picture shows. Build each of the circuits to test your predictions. Then, experiment to correct each of the faulty circuits. You may come up with other workable fixes, but you'll find one set of solutions on page 38.

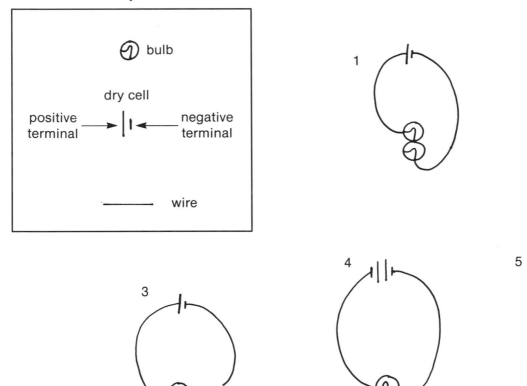

Conclusion

The experiments you conducted were a fun, safe way to begin investigating electricity. And now you may want to read more about it. You could look for books about how nuclear energy, water power, wind, and even solar energy are used to generate electricity. You might want to find out about the experiments performed by some of the early investigators of electricity, such as Alessandro Volta, Benjamin Franklin, Luigi Galvani, and Michael Faraday. Or you could find out how electricity is used to make the telephone, the radio, the television, and many other things work. Have you ever counted how many things you use in just one day that need electricity to run, produce light, or give off heat?

Electricity is an amazing force. Remember, though, it can also be dangerous. So think of ways you would like to investigate electricity. But only perform those experiments, like the ones in this book, that you can be absolutely sure are safe to try.

Circuit Solutions:

Circuit 2 will light. While you may have discovered other fixes, here are ways to make each of the faulty circuits work.

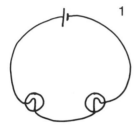

1

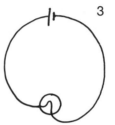

3

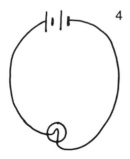

4

5

Index

Aluminum wire, 6
Argon, 12
Atoms, 1–2

Batteries, 2
Bulb
    burned out, 8
    and Edison, 8–9
    grain-of-wheat, 15
    incandescent, 10–13
    lighting up, 4, 7
    odd, 15–16
    search, 14
Circuits, 2
    challenge, 24–25
    complete, 4, 6
    crazy, 23
    faulty, 18
    in parallel, 26
    in series, 26
    short, 16, 32
    sleuths, 36
    symbols, 36
    tester, 19, 20
Columbia, S.S., 9
Conductor, 2, 19
    deduction, 21
Connections, 25–28
Contact points, bulb, 7
Copper wire, 6

Democratic Convention, 35
Dragon, 28
Dry cell, 2, 4
    in producing electricity, 5–6

Edison, Thomas Alva, 8–9
Electric current, 2, 5

Electricity, 1–2
    and bulb lighting up, 7
    dry cell in producing, 5–6
Electric Light's Diamond Jubilee, 15
Electromagnets, 33
Electromotive force, 6
Electrons, 1–2, 5–6

Faraday, Michael, 37
Filament, 7
Flashlight
    fun with, 30
    homemade, 29
Floats, for lights-on parade, 28
Foil wires, 3
Franklin, Benjamin, 37
Friction, 7
Fuse, 30–33
Fuse box, 32

Galvani, Luigi, 37
Grain-of-wheat bulb, 15

Incandescent bulb, 8–9
    manufacture of, 10–13
Insulators, 19

Lights-on parade, 28

Maglev, 22
Manganese dioxide, 5–6
Manganese oxide, 5
Morse, Samuel, 34, 35
Morse code, 35

Neutrons, 1
Nitrogen, 12
Nucleus, 1

Parade, lights-on, 28
Parallel connection, 26
Pete's dragon, 28
Polk, James K., 35
Protons, 1
Puppet show, shadow, 30

Resistance, and friction, 7
Ribbon machine, 11

Sealing and exhaust machine, 11–12
Separation layer, dry cell, 6
Series connection, 26
Shadow puppet show, 30
Shells, 1–2
Short circuit, 16, 32
Superconductors, 22

Switch, 33
Symbols, circuit, 36

Telegraph, 34
    and news flash, 35
Thermostat, 33
Train, and superconductor, 22
Tungsten, 9, 11
Vacuum, 8, 10, 12
Van Buren, Martin, 35
Volt, 6
Volta, Alessandro, 7, 37

Wires, foil, 3

Zinc, 5–6